W9-AXO-326

This book belongs to

_____

GOOFY SHAPES UP

Published by Advance Publishers
Winter Park, Florida

© 1997 Disney Enterprises, Inc.
All rights reserved. Printed in the United States.
No part of this book may be reproduced or copied in any form
without written permission from the copyright owner.

Written by Suzanne Weyn   Edited by Bonnie Brook
Penciled by Don Williams   Painted by H.R. Russell
Designed by Design Five
Cover art by Peter Emslie
Cover design by Irene Yap

ISBN: 1-885222-84-X
10 9 8 7 6 5 4 3 2 1

One morning Goofy said to his son Max, "I've decided to run in the Scrooge McDuck Marathon Race again."

"But, Dad," Max said, "remember last year? You couldn't even finish the race."

"That's because last year I was out of shape," Goofy told him. "This year I'm going to start working out right now, so I'll be nice and ready!" Goofy leaned down to pick up his barbell.

"Yoo-hoo!" someone shouted. It was Minnie Mouse. "Now wait just a minute. You can't lift something heavy without warming up your muscles first."

"Muscles?" Goofy asked. "I don't understand."

"You use muscles every time you move," said Minnie.
"Before you exercise, you should slowly stretch the
muscles first. Now follow me. Bend and stretch."

When they were done, Minnie said, "Now you're ready to exercise. And so am I. So long."

Goofy returned to his barbell and lifted it with ease. But while Goofy held it in the air, Max noticed that it started to bend.

"Dad! That barbell's made out of rubber!" Max cried.

Goofy blushed with embarrassment. "A-hyuk," he chuckled. "I thought I'd start out with something easy. I didn't want to strain my muscles."

"Right you are," said Mickey Mouse, coming into the yard. "Did you know your heart's a muscle, too?"

"My heart?" asked Goofy.

"Sure," Mickey replied. "The heart is a very strong muscle. It pushes blood all through your body. A good way to warm it up is by jumping rope."

"Have fun," Max said as he went back into the house.

Goofy jumped and jumped.
Suddenly he lost his grip
on one end of the rope.
"Yipes!" he shouted as his
jump rope wrapped around
him. "Help me! I think this
thing is alive!"

Goofy gasped. "Golly, my heart is pounding."

"That's because it was working extra hard," Mickey explained. "You should rest now."

"Sorry, nope, can't rest," Goofy objected. "I've got to exercise. I don't even have time to eat lunch."

"No lunch!" someone shouted. Mickey and Goofy turned to see who was coming.

Daisy Duck hurried into the yard. "You can't exercise without eating," she said. "You need energy, and energy is what you get from eating healthy foods."

She spread a blanket on the lawn and began taking food from her basket.

Goofy looked over the fruits, vegetables, breads, and meats Daisy had laid out. "Mmm!" he said, as he took a big bite of a sandwich.

When he had finished eating, Goofy thanked Daisy.

"You're welcome," Daisy replied, packing up her picnic basket and heading out of the yard.

"Time to jog," Goofy said. "Hic . . . hic . . . hiccup!"

"Uh-oh," said Mickey. "You have the hiccups. I bet you ate too fast. Next time, chew your food more slowly."

"Not a problem," Goofy assured Mickey. "I know a cure for hiccups. I'll just hold my breath as I run." Goofy took a deep breath and held it as he jogged out onto the sidewalk.

"Goofy," Mickey called. "I don't think that's a good idea." Goofy didn't hear him. He was already down the block.

Goofy jogged along holding his breath. Soon, he began to feel weak and dizzy. Then, all at once, he fainted.

Luckily, Mickey's nephews, Morty and Ferdie, were on their way to school. They stopped to help Goofy.

Slowly, Goofy's eyes fluttered open. Then he grinned. "Hey, my hiccups are gone! Holding my breath worked!"

"You can't hold your breath and run!" Morty cried. "That's why you fainted."

"Huh?" Goofy said.

"Air contains oxygen," Ferdie explained. "When we breathe, we bring air into our lungs."

"If you don't breathe, then you don't get oxygen," added Morty. "That's why you fainted."

"Well, whaddya know," said Goofy.

As Goofy waved good-bye to Morty and Ferdie, Scrooge McDuck drove up to the curb. "I hear you're entering my race again this year," he said to Goofy. "The prize is a brand-new bike."

"Wow! Max would love a new bike!" Goofy cried.

"Good luck," Scrooge McDuck said as his car pulled away. "You'll be up against the fastest runners in town."

"Whoa! The fastest runners in town?" Goofy repeated.
Suddenly he felt discouraged. "Who am I kidding? I'm
just not good enough to win that race. I might as well
not even try," he said glumly, sitting on the curb.

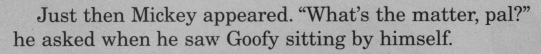

Just then Mickey appeared. "What's the matter, pal?" he asked when he saw Goofy sitting by himself.

"I'll never be able to win this race," Goofy mumbled. "I don't have what it takes."

"I know what your problem is," Mickey told him. "It's your brain."

"My brain?" Goofy gasped. "What do you mean? I thought it was working fine."

"Well, sure," said Mickey. "You're thinking, you're moving, you're breathing, and your heart is pumping. Your brain controls all those things and more."

"Then what's wrong with my brain?" Goofy asked.

"Your brain also controls your feelings," Mickey said. "A winning attitude comes from your brain."

"What's a winning attitude?" Goofy asked.

"It's the feeling that helps you to say, 'I can do it!' "

A slow smile spread across Goofy's face. "Listen, brain," he said. "I can do it! Hear that?"

"Good for you!" Mickey cheered.

For the rest of the summer, Goofy held onto his winning attitude. He trained hard, and did what he needed to do to keep himself strong and healthy.

Every morning after exercising, Goofy showered. Keeping clean helped fight germs that could have made him sick.

Just as Daisy had advised, he ate healthy foods.

He also drank
plenty of water.
When he exercised,
Goofy sweated.
Sweat was water
coming out of his skin.
By drinking, he put
back the water his
body needed.

He also went to bed early
so he would get enough sleep.

On the morning of the race, Minnie Mouse knocked on Goofy's front door.

"Surprise!" she said. "I brought you a present."

"For me?" Goofy asked, delighted. "What for?"

"It's a good-luck gift," Minnie explained.

"Wow, thanks!" Goofy cried when he opened the box and looked inside. "Sneakers—the nicest sneakers I've ever had."

"Your feet are important," said Minnie. "Especially when you're running a race."

"I have a good-luck gift for you, too," Max said from the stairs. "It's a visor to shield your eyes from the sun."

"Why, thank you, son," said Goofy. "Good thinking."

Next, Goofy got dressed and ate a healthy breakfast. He was already on the porch, when he stopped short. "Wait a minute. I forgot one thing," he said. "My winning attitude." He went back inside and looked in the mirror. "I can do it!" he said to his own reflection.

At the race, Goofy lined up with the
other runners. "On your marks,"
shouted Scrooge McDuck, "get set, go!"

Goofy ran as fast as he could. He was in the lead!

"Go, Goofy! Go, Goofy!" his friends cheered from the sidelines.

Suddenly, Goofy's visor fell over his eyes. He couldn't see. "Whoa! Who turned out the lights?" he shouted.

"Oops!" Goofy said as he tripped and fell over a rock. "Yeow!" he cried. He had scraped his knee.

Mickey and Minnie rushed to his side.

Minnie washed the cut. "When you tear your skin, germs can get in," she explained. "Soon you'll grow a scab over the cut, which is like your body's own bandage. But it's still a good idea to put a bandage over the cut to protect it."

Mickey helped Goofy to his feet. "Do you think you broke any bones?" he asked.

Goofy tested his legs and arms. "I think I'm all right," he said.

"Too bad you can't finish the race," Mickey said sadly.

"Who says I can't?" Goofy shouted. "Sure, my knee hurts. But I've got a winning attitude. Watch me go!"

Goofy started running again. His pals shouted and cheered. He ran up hills and down hills. He leaped across a mud puddle, and bounded over a boulder.

He caught up with the
other runners. Then he
passed them! Once again,
he was in the lead.

The finish line came into
view. Goofy was almost there!

"Nothing can stop me now," he thought. "Nothing
except — " Uh-oh, one of his shoelaces had come untied.

Just then, he stepped on the lace and stumbled.

Then he tripped and stumbled again — right through
the finish line ribbon!

"The winner is Goofy!" shouted Scrooge McDuck.

"Hooray for Goofy!" his friends cheered.

"Gawrsh," said Goofy, "it was nothing. I owe it all to my body — and a winning attitude!"